For Michael, with
all my love forever x
- CF

For Ali and Billie,
two brave ants
- CP

SIMON & SCHUSTER

First published in Great Britain in 2020 by Simon & Schuster UK Ltd, 1st Floor, 222 Gray's
Inn Road, London, WC1X 8HB • A CBS Company • Text copyright © 2020 Claire Freedman
Illustrations copyright © 2020 Claire Powell • The right of Claire Freedman and Claire
Powell to be identified as the author and illustrator of this work has been asserted by
them in accordance with the Copyright, Designs and Patents Act, 1988
All rights reserved, including the right of reproduction in whole or in part in any form
A CIP catalogue record for this book is available from the British Library upon request
ISBN: 978-1-4711-8148-1 (PB) • ISBN: 978-1-4711-8150-4 (eBook)
Printed in China • 10 9 8 7 6 5 4 3 2 1

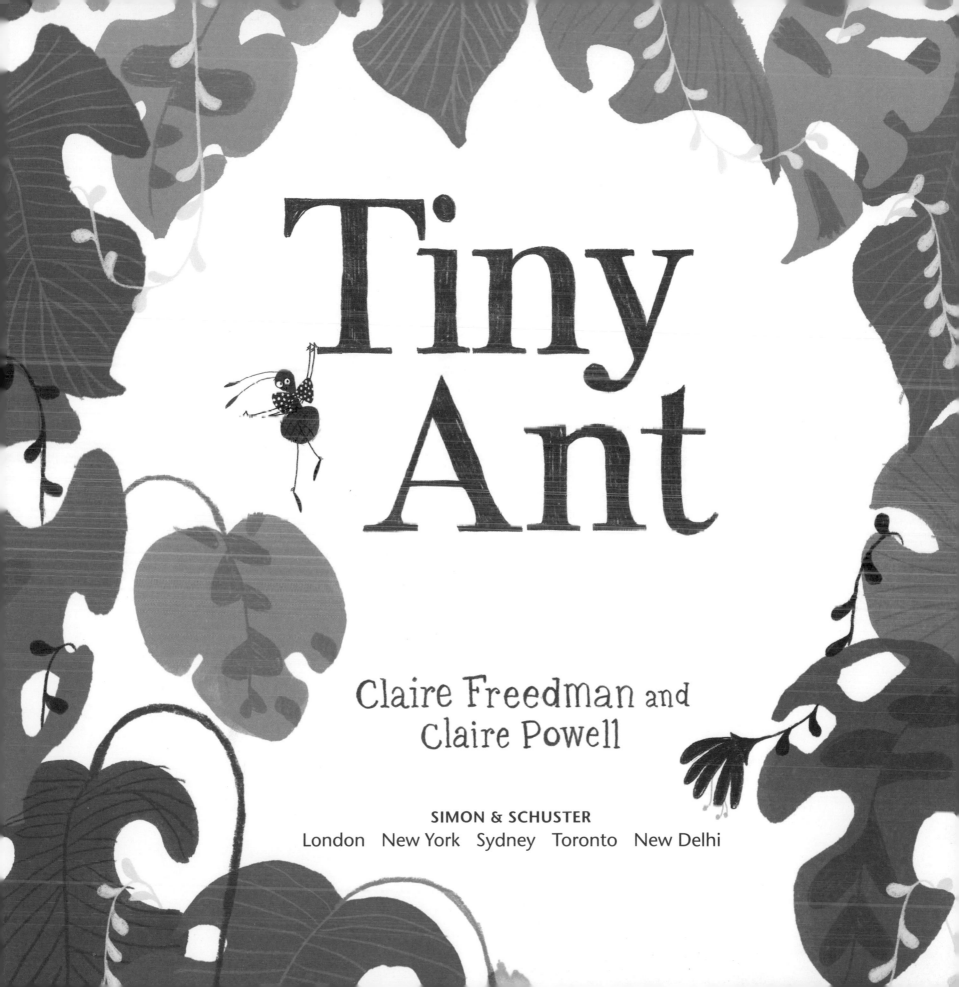

Tiny Ant

Claire Freedman and Claire Powell

SIMON & SCHUSTER
London   New York   Sydney   Toronto   New Delhi

In the jungle there's a contest
For the animals each year,

It's the show **Jungle's Got Talent**
And today it's filming here!

The animals rehearse their acts,
Whilst waiting in the queue,

They all LONG to be superstars,

Here's ANT!
What can HE do?

"Perhaps he's Mighty Muscle Ant!"
The others joke and jeer,

But Tiny Ant stands quietly,
Pretending he can't hear.

The judges strut and take their seats,
It's up to them who wins.

The audience go wild and clap,
At last the show begins . . .

First on the stage is Elephant,
He gulps a nervous cough,

Then shakes with fear,
Bursts into tears,

And has to be helped off!

It's Lion's acrobatics next,

Oh no!
His costume's split!

He's walking VERY oddly,

As he makes
a quick exit!

The Chipmunks introduce each act,

And hug them
if they're sad,

"You did your best!"
they tell them,

When the judges' score is bad!

The audience duck for cover:
Monkey's juggling act goes wrong!

POOH!
Smelly skunk is booed off stage,

He makes an awful pong!

The judges sigh and shake their heads, "This whole show is a bungle.

We've not one single animal,

With talent in this jungle!"

But lastly, out comes Tiny Ant,
He takes the microphone.

"I'm here to sing!"
Ant whispers.

"If you must," the judges groan.

Ant clears his throat,
opens his mouth,

His voice
rings crystal clear.

"SO beautiful!" the judges gasp,

And wipe away a tear!

"Oh wow!" the audience applaud,
They all stand up to cheer,

"It shows you can't judge anyone
By how they may appear!"

Ant wins the show and takes his prize,
It's been an awesome night.

Let's just hope no-one treads on him,
As he walks home tonight!

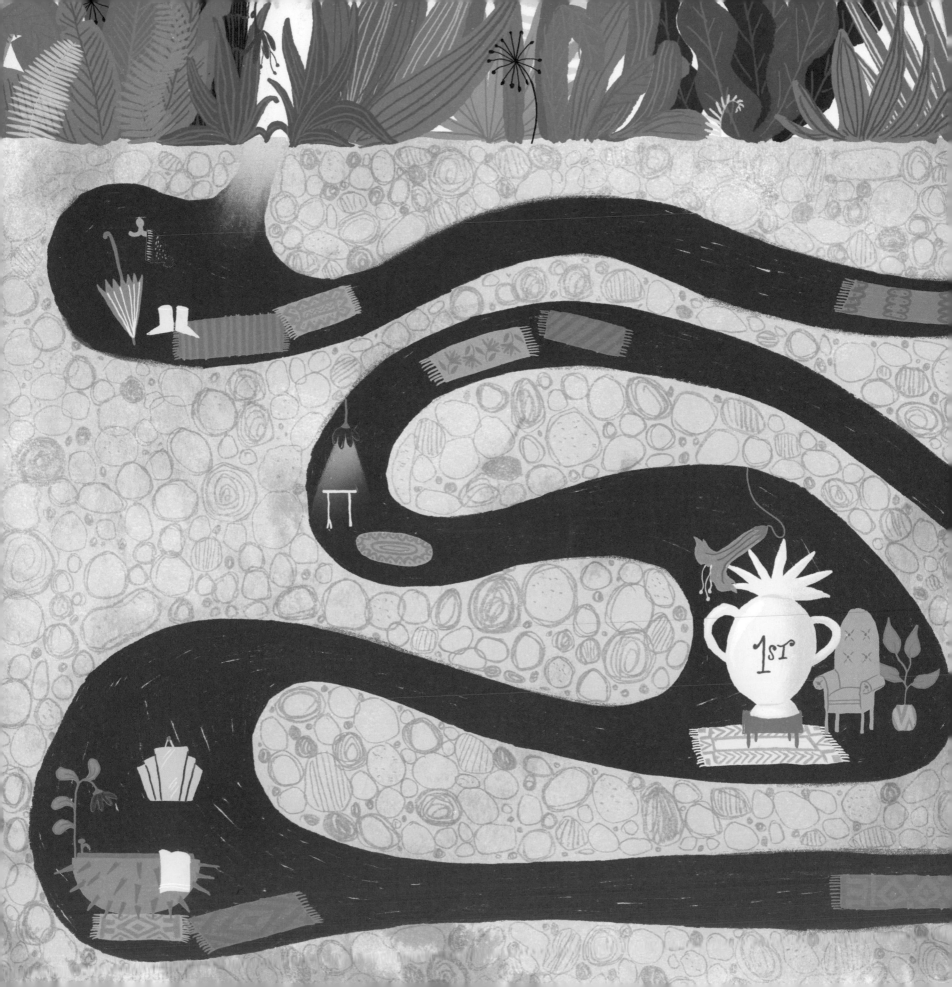